THE
ANCIENT FOREST

OUTER
SPACE

EMERALD
GLEN

GIANTS' TOWN

RICKETY
BRIDGE

THE
STINKY
SWAMPS

GOLDEN
COVE

For Jane and Emma,
my Christmas pixies
R.F.

For Jessica
C.C.

LADYBIRD
An Imprint of Penguin Random House LLC, New York

Written by Rhiannon Fielding. Text copyright © 2019 by Ladybird Books Ltd.
Illustrations copyright © 2019 by Chris Chatterton. All rights reserved.
First published in the United Kingdom in 2019 by Ladybird Books Ltd.
First published in the United States of America in 2020 by Ladybird, an imprint of
Penguin Random House LLC, New York. Manufactured in China.

Visit us online at www.penguinrandomhouse.com.

Library of Congress Cataloging-in-Publication Data is available upon request.

ISBN 9780241484708

10 9 8 7 6 5 4 3 2 1

TEN MINUTES TO BED

Little Unicorn's Christmas

Rhiannon Fielding · Chris Chatterton

One **cold winter evening** that glittered so bright,

in a forest that sparkled with magical light,

Twinkle the Unicorn pranced through the trees . . .

for that very night it would be
Christmas Eve.

The setting sun turned to a golden-pink glow,
but Twinkle was still rolling around in the snow.

"Ten minutes to bed!"
called her dad with a sigh . . .

but something above her
had caught Twinkle's eye.

It couldn't be Santa Claus's sleigh . . .
bedtime was still nine minutes away!
But with jingling bells, and a crash and a sneeze,
something huge landed
among the tall trees.

Into the glade came a man dressed in red,
with a fluffy white beard, and a hat on his head.
"Eight minutes to bed!" said the man with a shiver.

"And hundreds
of presents still
left to deliver!"

"One of my **reindeer** – can you guess who? –
is tucked in at home with a case of the flu.

Seven minutes to bed
– I'm afraid I'm quite slow –

and we've still got twenty-two
countries to go!"

He whistled and, suddenly, standing right there

was a **sleigh** and **eight reindeer**, all snorting the air.

Santa Claus was here – it was real! It was true!

With six minutes to bed
Twinkle knew what to do.

There was Dasher and Dancer, then Prancer and Vixen,
Comet and Cupid, then Donner and Blitzen . . .
with **Twinkle the Unicorn**
leading the way!

"Five minutes!" called Dad.

"Good luck, little sleigh."

Soaring along, then swooping down low,

over oceans and mountains all covered in snow,

with four minutes to bed, the sleigh traveled fast,
powered by unicorn glitter at last!

Each time they stopped, with clattering hooves,
and landed on boulders, or islands, or roofs,

Santa dropped off the presents
then called out the time:

"Three minutes to go, team!
Up, up! Time to shine!"

As they drew close to the last of the stops,
Twinkle caught sight of some leafy treetops.
"Two minutes to bed," Santa said with a wink . . .

"We couldn't have done it without you, young Twink."

From his sack he pulled out a **small gift** wrapped in red;

he gave it to Twinkle, then patted her head.

"One minute to bedtime – that goes for us, too!"

And with one final jingle,
away the sleigh flew.

Tucked into bed, as she closed her tired eyes,
Twinkle pictured great oceans, and rivers, and skies.
And soon she was sleeping and deep in her dreams,

on the soft leafy ground,
under silver moonbeams.

THE·LAND·OF
NOD

THE
BLACK
MOUNTAIN

THE
FLOATING
ISLANDS

SNOWY
VILLAGE

ENCHANTED
VALLEY

CREEPY
CASTLE

GLOOMY
DEN

BOULDER
GORGE

GLITTER
BAY